NORMAN BRIDWELL

Clifford's
FIRST VALENTINE'S DAY

SCHOLASTIC INC.
New York   Toronto   London   Auckland   Sydney
Mexico City   New Delhi   Hong Kong   Buenos Aires

For Courtney Noelle Patterson

ISBN-13: 978-0-590-92162-6
ISBN-10: 0-590-92162-2

Copyright © 1997 by Norman Bridwell.
All rights reserved. Published by Scholastic Inc.
SCHOLASTIC and associated logos are trademarks and/or
registered trademarks of Scholastic Inc.
CLIFFORD and CLIFFORD THE BIG RED DOG are
registered trademarks of Norman Bridwell.

38 37 36 35 34 33   8 9 10 11 12/0

Printed in the U.S.A.   23
First Scholastic printing, January 1997
Colorist: Manny Campana

Wheee! That's me, Emily Elizabeth, playing with my friends and my big red dog, Clifford.

We're excited because it's almost time for Valentine's Day.

Guess who always gets the biggest valentine?

Before Clifford grew up, he was a very small puppy.
He had a lot of adventures when he was little.
I'll never forget his first Valentine's Day.

It all started a few days before the holiday.
I was making valentines for Mommy, Daddy, Grandma,
and Grandpa.

Clifford wanted to help.
I gave him some paper.

He had his own way of cutting out hearts.

In those days we used white paste to stick
decorations on our valentines.
Clifford liked the smell of the paste.

He thought it would be good to eat.

He was wrong.
I had to wash out his mouth.

But I didn't see the paste all over his paws.
Oh-oh!

What a sticky mess!

After I had cleaned up my sticky red puppy,
we finished the valentines.
Clifford liked the special card I made for Grandma.

I wanted to mail it right away.

We got ready to take the card to the post office.

It was cold outside,
but I made sure Clifford stayed nice and warm.

When we got to the post office,
I pulled down the door to the mail chute.

Oh-oh. Clifford lost his balance.
He disappeared into the dark hole...

...and came out in the basement mailroom.

He sank down under a ton of letters in the cart.
The postal workers didn't see him.

MAIL SORTING ROOM

PROPERTY
U.S. POSTAL
SERVICE

Poor Clifford. He struggled and struggled, trying to get out — but he just kept slipping deeper and deeper.

Mommy and I told the postmaster what had happened.

He took us to the mailroom.

He said we could look for our puppy there.

How would we ever find Clifford?

Suddenly we heard a sound.

The mail was barking!
We dug into the letters as fast as we could.

Clifford was glad to see us.

And we were glad to have him back.

On Valentine's Day, I got a lot of cards.
I loved the one Grandma sent.

But the best valentine of all was from Clifford.

He will always be my favorite valentine.